The Uncanny Love of Jimmy Panagakos

Beth Hill

First published by Busybird Publishing 2015

ISBN (Print): 978-1-925260-80-9
ISBN (Ebook): 978-1-925260-81-6

Cover image: Kev Howlett
Cover design: Busybird Publishing
Layout and typesetting: Busybird Publishing

Busybird Publishing
PO Box 855
Eltham Victoria
Australia 3095
www.busybird.com.au

For Daniel

Pygmalion's marvelling soul was inflamed with desire for a semblance of body.
Again and again his hands moved over his work to explore it.
Flesh or ivory? No, it couldn't be ivory now!
He kissed it and thought it was kissing him too.
He talked to it, held it, imagined his fingers sinking
Into the limbs he was touching.

– Ovid
Orpheus' Song: Pygmalion
Book 10, line 252–257

This grand road appears at a distance like an immense avenue of foliage and verdure. A charming freshness and an agreeable shade always prevail in this continuous bower, the silence of which is interrupted only by the singing and chirping of the richly plumed parroquet and other birds which inhabit it.

– Francois Peron describing Parramatta Road in 1802.

Contents

Prologue

Sticky tape and rusted wire hold Jimmy's Milk Bar together. The windows are broken and pearled with dust. Makeshift bandages of wood and cardboard obscure the view inside.

Jimmy is always there; he keeps the milk bar open late into the night with the lights off. Standing behind the counter in the shadows. He is waiting, they say, for his dead brother to come back.

Some say maybe he did it, killed his brother. Others reckon Jimmy only came back to the milk bar after his brother had died to take up the inheritance their parents left them. Some say it's a drug front – you can buy smack from Jimmy if you know the right code words.

The lights are always out. The empty vinyl seats wait for no one.

Maybe he's just too poor to pay the power bill. People also say that his wife left him and took all the money. But maybe he never had a wife.

Nobody really knows why he stands there. People don't stop and look for long. People are quick and mean.

The faded red writing above the door says, *Come in now for tea*.

For tea?

Nobody goes to Parramatta Road for anything if they can help it.

The Milk Bar
2003

George lurches down the broken footpath of Parramatta Road. Fat drops of rain roll off his bald scalp and down past the yellowed back of his shirt collar. The drain down the hill is blocked with the usual crap – plastic bags, McDonalds wrappers and rotting leaves – so that the gutter is rapidly flooding. Late-night trucks thunder past, and splash dirty water onto his face. The telegraph poles arch at the stroke of their headlights and a red neon sign glows hot in his mind – a red neon *Asian 99* that fills his dick with blood and trips him up on the uneven path. Virgin wedding dresses sneer at him from the dark windows of storefronts.

He stumbles onward, under garish signs that do not match the dilapidated stores underneath them. The Thai restaurant that boasts a fine array of cardboard boxes instead of customers, the long-closed butcher shop where dusty plastic lettuce is still lit up in old refrigerator displays after five years. The old Bonds underwear shop-cum-Mexican restaurant, now a miscellaneous empty building with ratbags squatting inside, or maybe just the actual rats.

George stops at the old milk bar. What a pile of shit. One more turd along the avenue of shitty turds. The domain of sad idiots and degenerate fools. It fucking killed him, because he knew it could be more. He could turn it around if someone'd just listen to him.

He vomits pizza and beer into the milk bar's doorway. Pulling down his waistband he pisses on the doorstep for good measure and spits across the cracked window front.

Out from nowhere a broom knocks George across the side of the head, and he falls clumsily, grabbing at air on his way down. He hits the ground hard, face wet with blood, or is it rain? Urine? He retches again, doubled up on the concrete.

Jimmy leaves him lying there to fill a bucket with hot water and bleach. On his knees with a toothbrush he scrubs the cracks between her tiles. The stink fills his nostrils, twisting sharp in bowels that threaten to give way. He knows he is the very stuff he scrubs. Shame rises in his throat and his own snot falls and mixes with the bleach, with the vomit, the urine.

But he feels the intensity of her stare and knows he is forgiven. She turns his scrubbing into something beautiful – an act of devotion.

The way she opened her arms to everyone had once inspired a kind of admiration on his part. She was so accepting. People lit up in her glow. Everyone felt welcome and interesting. She shared herself with strangers. Jimmy had found it harder to accept that she opened her legs with a similar abandon, but he was in love with her. They had found peace together and those who had not understood had fallen away.

Hadn't the world started this way? Hadn't there been a time when there was no difference – hot, cold, hard, soft, sky and sea and earth and bones and blood wrapped all together? When had human bones been ripped from the molten cracks of ancient rock? Jimmy didn't know. But his guts wrenched when he placed his hands against her cold walls and felt the gap between skin and stone.

George stirs and rolls over, eyeing Jimmy with a slippery mixture of spite and regret.

'This is why you should sell your property, Jimmy. Fucking rough dickheads 'round here at night.' George coughs and spits. It's his way of laughing. 'You can't be making much money since they closed the cinema. And you weren't exactly making a mint when it was open, mate. Come on, why don't you sell her to me? I'll give you a good price. I'll turn her into something special, some classy apartments where rosy-cheeked kids can lie on the carpet and watch TV.'

Jimmy's knees ache. He turns, his back stiff, to squint at the man lying on the ground. The growing sense of recognition in his mind creeps in slowly like a thief to take his last scraps of dignity.

'You can't have her, George. Now fuck off.'

The Hills Hoist
2003

Ella can smell smoke. It reminds her of last summer, and the summer before that. Reminds her of every bloody summer she's ever known. Quite frankly, she is over life in this numb back garden. Seventeen. She should have better things to do than sit at the top of the Hills Hoist and spy on the next-door neighbours screaming at each other.

Fuck all ever happened here. Fuck all ever happened in her own life. The wogs dug veggie gardens and the yuppies moved in together, renovated the kitchen, banged out snot-kids and wore Birkenstocks to buy their milk and tofu in the mornings.

From the top of the washing line Ella can see the back gardens of the whole street and more beyond the back alleyway. Gardens on their side of the street are mostly the same – concrete, full of old rubbish, rusting cars, plastic garden furniture, a patch of grass if the owners are especially botanical, everything dim grey in the city night glow. Families like theirs, who clung to the curve of Parramatta Road, houses whose front doors were the storefronts – well, they were different. Different from the gardens across the back alley, the ones with water installations and native plants.

She's got plans to get out of here soon. Maybe after she finishes Year 12, maybe before. She dreams of trees and mountains and blue sea horizons in tiny towns where nobody's ever heard of Parramatta Road, or her dad, and especially not of Aunty Fi.

The whining of her aunty's sewing machine – as if on cue – cuts through her bush-dreaming and reminds her how far she is from leaving. How guilty she'd feel leaving Aunty Fi alone here with nothing but the sewing machine for company. Ella hears the slam of the side gate. George joins her in the garden for his evening cigarette.

'Get down from there,' he grumbles. 'You know how spying pisses off the neighbours.'

'Yeah right. Where've you been?' Ella senses

the cloud of alcohol blurring the edges of her father's words. She smells the hint of piss and vomit.

'Drinking.'

Drinking. As always. Drinking and obsessing over his crazy plan. She can't understand it, his ridiculous plan to buy the row of shitty shops down from their own, knock them down and build something equally shitty in their place. Like he thinks that's going to turn the whole road around. Can't he see it doesn't matter what he builds there? The rest of the sane population gave up on Parramatta Road fifty years ago when the cars took over. It's dead, and no amount of fresh paint will bring it back to life. That's why she'd rather leave the whole thing behind her. Find a place with no roads, a place where she belongs.

Broomie
1955

Anthea braced herself against the bright heat of the sun as she pushed hard into her front door. It was stuck again, swollen against the frame in the humidity. Sweat rolled down Anthea's legs, pooling in her heavy factory work shoes.

The door gave way beneath her weight and swung into the cool darkness of the hallway. A child stood in front of her, something in her hands. Startled at Anthea's sudden entrance, the child's hands came apart. The something – Anthea's vase, she recognised it now – smashed on the floor. Anthea felt time pass through her, breaking her as surely as the vase that now lay in ugly terracotta pieces at her feet.

A moment earlier her past had been graspable. Made from the clay of her ancestor's riverbeds, chipped on the corner from the time Yiayia knocked it on the kitchen doorframe of their old house in Kypseli. The vase was one of the few things they had decided to bring with them when they left Greece. Now all that was gone. Perhaps it had been gone for a long time. She could never have that time back. She would never again lean against the soft worn wood of that kitchen doorframe while Mama cooked dinner.

The girl's hands were frozen around the shape where the vase had been. The howl from Anthea's lungs seemed to come from the walls themselves.

From the kitchen where he was looking for some foil to make a crown for their game, Jimmy knew he would be in trouble.

He tiptoed up the hallway, clutching Broomie to his chest. He did not want the sound of his feet to add to the turmoil; he did not want Mama to see him. He knew who would be blamed for this and his bum was still raw from his last hiding for keeping the little broom under his pillow. But now Broomie would come in handy. Together they could sweep away the mess that was making Mama so sad. He brushed his hands through the black bristles for reassurance.

Mama's body, bent over the broken vase, was backlit by the hot summer day blaring through the open door. Her face was in shadow and he could not make out her expression. He held the broom out. A peace offering.

'It wasn't Fi's fault, Mama.'

'Of course it was her fault.'

'I can help clean it up, Mama, make it good as new. No more mess.'

Anthea picked up a larger piece of the vase. Then she threw it to the ground. Its gratifying crash was not unlike the smash of plates at her wedding.

'Where is your mother?' Anthea asked the little girl.

Jimmy stepped closer again and began sweeping up the mess. Anthea dropped another piece of the vase; Jimmy stopped sweeping.

'Where is your mother?' She shouted it now. Her mouth, clumsy with humiliation, strained to form the words in English. 'Where is her mother, Dimitri?'

Jimmy winced. She only used his Greek name when he was in a lot of trouble.

Anthea smashed another piece of the vase. It felt good to take control. It felt good to break something. Squatting, Anthea pressed her hands against the shards, crumbling them into smaller pieces. So small that anything that looked like her vase would be gone. Anything that reminded her of another time would be reduced to dust. She sliced the side of her palm on one of the sharper pieces. Her blood fell in droplets, staining the dust of her own treasured past.

'They're in the garden, aren't they?' Anthea strode down the hallway to the back door. It was not really a question.

Jimmy watched, not knowing how to stop her or how he might clean it all up. Broomie was useless for liquids. Jimmy stroked the broom along his arm. The tickle of bristles against his skin was soothing; he loved the way the plastic blue handle fit in his palm just right.

Paralysed by indecision, he turned and brushed the broom over Fi's head, signalling it was safe to emerge.

'Sorry about my mum. She really liked that vase, I guess.'

Fi's cheeks were still wet from crying. 'I just thought it would be a good addition to our set of crown jewels.'

'It was a pretty dumb idea anyway.'

'Yeah.'

They both stared at the ground. Jimmy continued to run the brush up and down his arm.

'Stop doing that, Jimmy. It's weird.'

'I just brought it to help clean up!'

'Yeah, but it's weird.'

Before he could defend himself Fi's mum

appeared, her hands still covered in dirt from the garden and holding a plastic bag swollen with fresh potatoes. Without a word, she grabbed Fi and bustled her out the still-open front door.

Fi shouted as they rounded the front gate, 'Bye, Jimmy! Sorry about the vase. I hope you don't get in any trouble.'

Jimmy used a sponge from the kitchen to wipe up the mess. There were a few pieces of the vase still intact, one with the spindly orange leg of a dancer painted on it. He tucked the piece into his pocket. There must be something special about this vase the way the broom was special, otherwise Mama would not have gotten so upset about it.

So he wasn't the only one who had special things.

He could hear his parents arguing outside and hoped his brother Paul would get back from soccer training soon. Paul was good at making everyone feel better. He guessed Papa didn't like Mama being such good friends with the vase, like he was with the broom. Papa really didn't like that at all.

Later that night, Anthea clanged the pots and pans from the stove to the sink because she knew how it irritated her husband. Michael sat at their kitchen table, dusting dirt off the creamy skin of his home-grown potatoes. She noticed that he caressed them the way he might have caressed her once, looking for comfort. But, now, she had endured too many dinners of mashed potato and carrot soup punctuated by romantic stories of her husband's childhood. The rolling green hills, the olive trees and the rich black soil began to take on qualities of God's Eden, and she, ever so gradually, was condemned to crawl on her belly in the dust of the city, to repent for the temptation that had led him astray.

Michael had been a farmer back in Greece. He had travelled halfway 'round the world chasing Anthea, and had forgotten the route back. He missed the smell of soil. In the city you can't smell soil, only dirt. Somewhere far underneath the pavement and the tar that moist, life-giving scent lay dormant, and he too felt buried in the shadows of enormous city buildings.

In the supermarket under bright lights Anthea would watch as Michael surreptitiously smelled the carrots and potatoes. Michael claimed that when he lifted them to his hairy nostrils he could hear their quiet sobs for their lost aroma. Anthea knew it was ridiculous to be jealous, but unlike his deliberate avoidance of her sorrow, she knew his affinity with the vegetables was total.

'You can't keep giving away all our vegetables like that, Michael.' Anthea did not look up from the pot she was cleaning.

'I was being generous.'

'You are too generous with this woman.'

He laughed. A risky strategy.

'It's good for business.' He paused and laughed again. 'It keeps our customers returning.'

'We have the boys to think about. You think I like to work so many shifts at the factory?'

'I think you like to be far away from me, yes.' His voice was calm.

Anthea turned from the sink now and slammed down the saucepan. She immediately regretted doing this. He always got to her. Michael, ever calm, sitting there cleaning his potatoes. His repetitive and gentle stroke stripped back her protective outer layer till she was raw and ready for the slicing.

'You could quit your job at the factory,' he said.

She had seen this coming. 'You could close the store.'

Their eyes locked.

'You know the store is all I have,' he said.

'Please. You want me to feel guilty now? Think about the boys.'

'The boys are fine. Jimmy has a friend in Fi; he hardly picks up the broom these days.'

'He had it this afternoon.'

'You scared him with the vase.'

'I scared him? Maybe he was wondering where his father was.'

'He knew I was out in the garden digging up potatoes with Fi's mother.'

'I remember when we dug up potatoes!'

'Calm down.'

'I'm not an idiot, Michael!'

'Finish the washing up. I have nothing more to say about this.'

From upstairs in Paul and Jimmy's bedroom it sounded, as always, as if their mother was arguing with herself. Her accusations echoed hollow through the house. Their father, soft-spoken, wielded a passive aggression that settled like dust on the emotional furniture of their lives. You could feel it in the air, but you could never hear it.

Jimmy had managed to smuggle Broomie to bed where it was now tucked comfortably under his arm. He would be in big trouble if he got caught again, but it was worth it.

He had first found the broom when he was looking in the kitchen cupboards for a saucepan to use as a drum. Broomie was bright blue and made of plastic, bristles thick and black. It fitted perfectly into place with a blue dustpan with a good click.

It was famous.

There was a giant billboard down the road from them where a beautiful blonde woman with eyes that popped stood in her bright white kitchen surrounded by cleaning products. In her hands between her shiny red fingernails was the striking blue handle of his very own friend.

Holding it in his own hand he felt somehow closer to her happy smile. *No Fuss Cleaning!* she proclaimed from her height above the trams and traffic.

He liked that.

Fi
1974

The glass was warmer than Jimmy expected. It felt good against his skin. He leaned his head against it to hear the music up loud. His breath fogged the clean window as he put his lips to it and made a face. That always made Fi laugh. His wet shirt was sticking cold against his back, his hair still dripping.

They made a cosy scene in there without him.

The light glowed tender from the orange lampshades hanging from the ceiling, illuminating Paul as he twirled Fi around, his back long and muscular so that she span easily beneath his arm. Laughing, her eyes slid past Jimmy's forlorn shadow at the window, her grace slippery and glittering.

Paul lifted her onto the bench top and pressed his thick lips into her face. Jimmy turned away. He stamped his feet up and down in a futile attempt to keep warm. Banging harder on the window and shouting, Jimmy watched as his brother's hands crept under Fi's light-blue cardigan.

Fiona squirmed – with delight or discomfort? Jimmy knew she could see him. He pressed his ear to the glass to catch their conversation.

'Paul, I … please Paul, just give me a, Paul … it's just that Jimmy—'

'Honey, Jimmy will be fine.'

'But—'

'He gets it, honey.'

'He's outside, Paul. He's stuck outside, he must've forgotten his key or something.'

Paul ambled slowly to the door and unlocked it.

Jimmy plonked himself at one of the tables. It was covered in crumbs and dried sticky rings left by messy milkshake drinkers. He brushed the crumbs into a pile.

'You guys were supposed to clean up tonight.'

'Well, we were. But we were waiting for you. You know how you like things done and I didn't think it was fair that Fi should clean up.'

'Didn't look like you were waiting for me.'

Fi smiled at him from the bench top, tucking

her hair behind her ears. She was flushed and fidgeting under the orange glare of light. 'We were, Jimmy. I was waiting for you.'

Jimmy rubbed his finger around a dried milkshake ring. Paul started the record player again and lifted Fi back onto her feet. She stood there for a moment, leaning against the bench

'Well, I suppose I should go anyway. It's pretty late.'

'No, you should stay. This won't take long. Come on. Help us out.'

Jimmy's eyes searched for hers. 'Stay for a bit. I didn't mean to be … I'm just really tired. No one mops a floor like you do, Fi.'

Fi laughed. 'What are we going to do with you, Jimmy Panagakos?'

Jimmy handed her the mop, grinning. 'You remember how to do that, don't you?'

'Of course.' Her chapped hands brushed past his, bitten fingernails tucked into her palms as she swung the mop backward and forward. Her hips moved to the music. Paul came up from behind and slid his hands into her jean pockets. She smiled a private smile that Jimmy knew too well.

Jimmy wondered how much longer it would last. Paul and Fi had been seeing each other for two months now. She was too good for him. Not that she knew it.

Fi had the self-conscious air that drew eyes

toward her. There was heaviness about her – no, it was more than that. There was something about her that drew the light inwards like those black holes Jimmy had read about. She craved that light.

Here between Paul and Jimmy it poured in and filled her. She was spectacular. The mirrors along the sidewall reflected her movement. The wooden floors shone wet beneath her feet. The situation was daily becoming more unbearable. Jimmy wanted to ram the mop hard into her gut again and again. From behind the counter Paul produced a bottle of the old homemade ouzo.

'A little something to pass the cleaning hour quicker.' He poured the ouzo into three milkshake glasses, and they drank.

Jimmy started as always by wiping down the counter top, attempting to ignore Fi, a retraction of affection his only means to punish her for a crime she was unaware of committing. His fingers moved lightly across the marbled plastic of the counter checking for any sticky patches missed. His affectation of concentration changed into a genuine focus on the delightful smoothness of the surface. His hands danced over and around each other. He felt the ouzo thawing his chest, moving up through his neck to his face so that sweat began to mingle with his damp shirt.

This was their space.

He felt giddy at the joy of it. The walls, recently painted bright yellow, cradled him with delight – their dreary days as mere background to vegetables and fruit were over. It was a guilty thought loosened by his dead father's ouzo.

Jimmy moved to the tables, turning his back on the lovers' retreat into the kitchen. Drinking and wiping, drinking again.

There was a knock at the front window. Janey wiggled her long fingers in his direction. Jimmy opened the door and let her inside.

'I was hoping you'd still be here. Where are Fi and Paul?'

'Oh, I think they went out the back to clean the kitchen.' Jimmy grinned with what he hoped was charm, knowing that his face came together like a poor imitation of his brother's.

Jimmy played his role with gusto. They moved to the side booth at the back of the store. Their tongues slid rhythmically against each other's. Away from the focus of cleaning, Jimmy's mind began to wander again. He imagined Paul and Fi out the back. The image of Paul's hands creeping underneath her cardigan was on replay. Jimmy pulled away from Janey and rubbed his eyes in an attempt to erase the image.

'Sorry.'

'That's fine.'

She lit a cigarette. They were both bored. Janey began to talk; the noise washed over him.

Her face was so close to his he could barely make out her features through the cigarette smoke.

He stared numbly through predictable tangents of her stories to the smudge on the front window. His heart, brimming with the torrent of alcohol, noticed a sad longing emanating from the glass.

His own smudge on the pane was like a small face pleading with him. Waiting to be seen. Recognised.

'So I said to her, you don't know what you're talking about … Jimmy?'

A small face watching him. Smiling even.

'Jimmy?'

How had he not noticed her before? His hands moved to the wall behind him. Leaning his back against it, reality pulsed through him. Beautiful, simple, here.

'You're pretty drunk, Jimmy.'

'What? I'm fine. You just caught me in the middle of cleaning.'

'I can help.'

'No that's fine; you should go.'

'But—'

'Great to see you though. I'll see you tomorrow night?'

'Yeah, um, I don't know.'

'Great. Bye.'

Deftly now, he moved her from the booth and out the front door onto the street. Closing the door behind her, his hands lingered at the handle and then squeezed.

'Found you.' Jimmy laughed, nervous and excited.

Thieves
2003

Cash Palace is where possessions come to die. A jumble of other people's memories. The bottom of the consumer food chain. Though you wouldn't know it from the way that George sweeps his arm around with pride as he explains the layout of the store to Tim, from the cabinets filled with tacky jewellery to the old stereos and novelty lamps.

Ella squats unnoticed behind the big display cabinet near the front door, wading through the stink of death, as she organises the objects inside. She hates it. All these things spat out with nowhere to go. Waiting fruitlessly like abandoned dogs for their owners to return. Not a friend in the world. Just the antiques buyers – mostly thieves with toffy accents. Whoring out the good furniture to keep the auction wheel turning. They won't buy the little girl's jewellery box with the dent on the corner, or the old ashtray that says, 'Love Linda 1986'. Ella's the only one who'll look after them now.

Tim nods along, apparently impressed by this collection, as George goes on about the historical value of these pieces, as if their shop is a museum or an art gallery. Ella's heard her dad's spiel before. Especially the loaded pauses. She fills them herself. Her father doesn't explain, for example, the way that fingertips can shed tears. She's seen it. The salty sweat of wrinkled hands that fumble old jewellery across the counter. He doesn't mention the junkies fidgety clutch when they're looking to sell whatever they can get their hands on for a bit of cash. Or the fat cleavage of the prostitutes who drop in from down the road to pawn the gold watch their latest customer 'left behind.'

Her dad never gives anyone their asking price.

'Never pay them what they ask,' he says. 'They aren't professionals. They're all, "my mother's this" and "I bought it for this much". People aren't too good at converting sentimental value into monetary terms, Tim. That's what *we're* here for.'

Her dad, the master of reincarnation. Everything can be born again. And then sold again at a very reasonable price.

Her father is up to the bit about shoplifters. 'It's the bloody mothers with prams you've gotta watch. Bored shitless, looking for a kick. They've got no business here. They can go and take that carry on to Kmart. I haven't got the time or inclination to deal with time wasters, or thieves.'

Unless the thieves are there to sell him something, thinks Ella.

Cash Palace. At least her dad named this place right.

Then George is gone to meet some associate for lunch, without an explanation of the cash register. Her chance. She steps out from her spot and accidentally sets the front buzzer off. Tim swaggers towards her, chest up.

'Good morning. How can I help you?' he says, as if he owns the place.

His hands are too big for his shoulders. Ella raises an eyebrow. 'I'm after something for my boyfriend. A bracelet.' She bats her blue mascara eyelashes, and the skin between his freckles goes pink. Tim paws around behind the cash register a little too frantically, looking for the keys. When he eventually locates them at the back of the bottom drawer and looks up again Ella is already standing at the cabinet with the unlocked glass door slid open.

Swearing under his breath, Tim swings the heavy keys around his fingers as he walks toward her.

'Must've forgotten to lock it last time.'

'You've got to be careful, hey?' Ella winks, but does not move from her spot between him and the glass pane of the cabinet.

'You want something in silver or gold?'

He steps closer, trying to reassert himself as the shop owner, and she presses her warm hand to his concave chest. Now they can both feel how hard his heart is beating. Ella smiles wide at this and presses her body up against him as her other hand slowly takes one of the gold bracelets out and fists it into her back pocket. Tim is breathing hard.

'Well, are you going to look in the cabinet or—?'

Ella turns to face the cabinet and pretends to look in great detail at each piece. Their bodies are separated now, but he's standing close behind her.

'Well, it's all a bit tacky anyway, isn't it?' she says, closing the cabinet door, and making sure the lock clicks into place.

She walks out and imagines Tim discovering the gap in the cabinet. Then she sees him trying every key on the ring to unlock the damn thing before George returns from lunch.

The illicit buzz of the successful heist vibrates

through Ella's body as she flees Cash Palace. But as her pulse returns to normal, paranoia sets in. Turning into the shady doorway of another store to catch her breath, she finds herself in the rubbery embrace of the rainbow plastic strips of Jimmy's Milk Bar. He is there, of course, a silhouette backlit by the fluorescent light of a storage cupboard. He acknowledges her presence by turning back to the cupboard, continuing his search for a piece of cardboard to cover the latest gaping addition to his front window.

The heat of summer has stripped him back to a yellowed singlet that hangs on his bony frame. He fingers and turns the different objects in the cupboard with a light caress, as if the old light fittings and chocolate boxes were fragile birds left in his care.

The store is narrow and dark. A long counter runs along the sidewall. Behind it shelves sag under ornate arrangements of chocolate bars long past their use-by date.

A small blue fan in the corner lamely circulates the clammy air. Ella has never dared to enter this place by herself, but now she is here she cannot leave without buying something, anything. Her curiosity bolts her fidgeting feet to the floor.

'I'd like a chocolate milkshake please,' she says to no one in particular. And then to Jimmy: 'Do you make chocolate milkshakes here?' He turns slowly away from the cupboard; his disembodied torso hovers toward the refrigerator. The blue fan answers her question with a mocking *click click*. She eyes the huge refrigerator at the back of the store with dread.

The whirring of the milkshake machine starts up and she uses the noise to move closer to the counter where he stands, not quite believing that he really stocks fresh milk in the big old refrigerator.

'Two dollars.'

She peers over the edge of the cup on the counter in front of her to check the brown froth. Fumbling through the pockets of her jeans she locates a dollar fifty and slides it across the counter. 'I'm sorry; I'm fifty cents short. I … didn't really plan to … I'll bring it with me next time.' She uses the last spasmodic trickles of her heist buzz to pull her head up and look him in the eye. 'Sorry.'

His eyes are deeply set in the shadow of his brow, and at first she can make out no discernable reaction. But then, slowly, her eyes now adjusted to the muted tones of the milk bar, she perceives a sort of sadness there, between his thick grey eyebrows. Something human that emanates from the otherwise ethereal shadow of his person, something she sort of recognises.

He breaks her gaze by looking down to the milkshake and pushing it towards her. Snatching up the money with his other hand he walks slowly out the door at the back of the shop, leaving her alone with the flickering light of the storage cupboard and the chocolate bars. She gulps in a mouthful of syrupy milk that tastes like her childhood and looks into the smiling faces of the faded 1960s Coca-Cola ad on the wall beside her.

For the first time since entering she breathes out and then in again. Free from Jimmy's creepy stare to do some real investigating. She traces the cold metal ribbing that surrounds one of the plastic table tops and wanders to one of the two pink booths near back of the store. So many empty tables. There is definitely a funny smell in the air, like something, somewhere in the building, is rotting.

Ella walks towards the front of the store now, where a chocolate-bar pyramid of epic proportions sits precariously in the front display. She can hardly imagine Jimmy's awkward shadow and thick hands managing to balance each bar on top of the other. Why would he take the time to create such an arrangement, and for who? Next to the pyramid there is a bucket of lollipops with wrappers yellowing like dying flowers. She reaches out to touch one, to see if it is real.

'Do not touch that.'

She finds him standing less than a metre away from her behind the counter. How long had he been standing there? Waiting silently. Watching her.

'You have finished your milkshake.'

It is a command to leave rather than an observation. She turns quickly to face him. Placing her milkshake down on the counter in front of him apologetically, she turns and leaves. The plastic strips cling to her t-shirt and slow her down.

She wants to look back at him, but she doesn't.

Of Flesh and Concrete
1974

Jimmy felt bold in the darkness. Who could really say where he ended and she began?

Her storeroom had no windows. He breathed in slowly. She smelt sweet. It was a tiny walk-in cupboard with shelves that began just above knee height and continued to the ceiling.

Jimmy used to crawl under the bottom shelf when he played hide and seek with Fi. It was always the last place Fi would look. Jimmy had enjoyed being curled up in the warm safety of the bottom shelf. Had the store noticed him even then?

It could be any time of day, but when you stood in here it felt like the middle of the night.

Jimmy closed the door softly behind him and leant into the shelves, pressing his hardened groin against her. He heard her gasp, her wooden shelves firm against his body, a solid and unwavering response that was so unlike the fleshy women who softened and yielded to his hesitant touch. He had hated the way they would cry out, or recoil, or worse when they gripped him and refused to let go.

He had not planned this, and in a way he had always been planning this. He felt exposed. Turning the lights out had stripped away the usual accidental nature of their interaction. His true intentions, his real feelings, so well veiled by the orange glow of business hours, now stood naked and shivering between them in the darkness. He leant harder against the jutting wood of her shelves.

Perhaps this time he would not slide away.

Perhaps this time he could really hold her.

Curled up under the bottom shelf, he had been so tiny then. The perfect spot. Too perfect. How long had he waited there to be found? Had it been an hour, or just ten minutes before the storeroom door opened and he'd seen the fraying stitches of a woman's sandals through his squinted lashes. Her feet had been smelly. Jimmy had watched the deep red cracks of decaying skin that opened and closed at her heels as she rocked back and forth, his father's yellowed trainers behind her.

Now his own shoes creaked at the eager swinging of his hips. Giddy and close to coming he could feel her excitement too, the rasping breath of wind in her roof, the groan of her foundations shifting. He gripped at her, tearing boxes down from the shelves. He wanted to go deeper somehow. He wanted to be inside of her, he wanted her inside of him.

He fumbled at his belt buckle. Unzipping his trousers and pulling down his underwear, he pushed himself up between the wall and a paper bag filled with chocolate powder. The wall was cold against his dick, thrilling but ambiguous to the hot throb of his body. He paused, uncertain once more.

He remembered another time, filled with doubt, when his body had begun to disobey him. As usual Paul had been in the bed opposite reading a comic book with a torch, the faded green bedspread shivering rhythmically at his groin. Jimmy had always pretended not to notice. But that night he found himself pushing harder into his own mattress, curled up with the sheets pulled over his head. His fingers had found his balls before he could stop them. They had pulled and tugged as images flicked through his mind. *Ankles, lips, thick black bristles.*

He had stopped, and opened his eyes to the dark green underside of his blanket. His breathing already too heavy, the lemon smell of freshly cleaned sheets had been nauseating. But his hands kept moving. Up toward the tip of his penis, they had rubbed and played. *Stomach, breasts, nipples, hard blue handle.*

He had stopped again, this time rubbing his eyes. He had rolled onto his stomach and jammed his hands under his pillow and waited for his unsated erection to subside. This had not been the first time. His mind and his penis had been in collusion for a while, wandering in directions he did not want to follow.

Now as an adult he traced between the bricks of her storeroom wall, the old doubt, fresh again as the memory of Broomie came back to him. Did she really want this? Would he ever know? His touch was light and inquiring. He needed her to trust him. He needed to trust himself. He began to move again, more slowly, drawing out their pleasure. He felt her respond; his fingertips trembled at the sudden surge of love from her walls.

Overwhelmed, warmth spread through his chest and down his stomach into his groin. He whimpered, falling to his knees so that pain shot up his thighs.

He cried out in agony and joy as he came.

At thirteen, he hadn't really understood. Broomie was his comfort, and his plaything. His secret friend. Instinctively that night he had reached down the side of his bed to where the old broom was lodged. The bristles were falling out and all bent to one side from being wedged down next to the wall. He had held it to his chest, its familiar handle in his palm. His breathing had slowed; the broom always had this calming effect. He had kept his eyes wide open a long time, watching the dark shadows that swept across the ceiling as the big tree outside their window was whipped from side to side by the midnight wind. Paul had fallen asleep by this time; Jimmy could hear him snoring softly. There was also the familiar muffled thunder of his father's snoring from the room across the hall. His mother had always been silent at this hour of the night. And he had imagined her, tossing and turning, unable to fall asleep as she so often complained. He had not been able to sleep either.

On his knees in the storeroom now he felt about all over the ground for the patch of wet. Could she forgive him his human stickiness? His shirt was damp and he shivered. The ejaculation had created a vacuum inside of him that his doubts were quick to fill. Had he broken their bond? Had he come too quickly? Was she unsatisfied? He was just a young man really; she was experienced, sophisticated, expected more. Was it his father she really craved? Was that why he used to bring his women here?

The memory of his final night with Broomie surged forward again. He remembers his body, curled up in his bed, his eyes wide open, his dick hard against his stomach. He had clutched the broom at his chest, his arm muscles tense with the effort of not moving. It had been a battle between his most intense desire and his sense of what was right. They had been friends so long, these needs, new and foreign, had crept across his mind and lingered longer than he had meant them to. He had known his sentiments were not returned, yet he badly wanted them to be. In the end it would be his choice.

It had been his choice.

He had moved his hand slowly upward so that his fingers were in between the frayed softness of its bristles. A moan had escaped his mouth. He had looked at Paul asleep and bit his lip to prevent any further noise. Gradually, he had lowered the broom across the flat of his stomach that trembled under its touch. The soft fuzz at the lower half of his abdomen had risen to greet the prickle of the broom, two different kinds of hair enmeshed briefly. Were they really so different?

He had pressed the broom briefly against his dick. Frantically now he began to rub it against his thighs, under his balls, and back up his stomach. In seconds he had come, warm thick goo through his fingers, through the beautiful black brush of the broom. There had been so much of it he could hardly believe it had come from him. He had not thought beyond that moment. He had forgotten the one thing he knew so well about his friend: Broomie was no good with liquids.

Sick with shame he had tiptoed to the bathroom to clean up. In the darkness he had removed his sodden pyjama pants and lifted his friend to the sink. His assault had left the black bristles stuck together and bent out at odd angles. He had cried hot tears as he washed it with the hand soap.

Broomie's handle had been rigid with disapproval.

Tonight in the storeroom his heart was racing; he had truly penetrated her. Maybe their love was possible. He dared to imagine their children. Then he located the warm liquid that had spurted from his penis. She had caught it with easy grace at the mouth of an open box of baked bean cans. His heart sank. He hated the sight of his own semen. Like a pool of grey snot, waiting for the wipe of a pitiful tissue. Something that gave him away.

That terrible scene in the bathroom had been exposed in a series of freeze frames as the florescent light sputtered to life. Flash. Skinny legs, naked. Flash. The broom under the stream of water in his hands. Flash. Striped pyjama pants in a crumpled heap on the floor. Finally the light had beamed to life. Jimmy dropped the broom as he grabbed his pyjama pants from the ground to cover his nakedness. For a moment his mother had been silent.

'What are you doing in here?' she had asked him pointlessly.

Now in the milk bar's store room he turned the light on to check he'd caught it all. He dreaded this moment, but he could not leave her without cleaning up. He was surprised to find the bright light cheerful. She relaxed at his touch. Part of the cardboard box was soggy. Well, there was nothing he could do about that. A part of her had absorbed him, their secret. For a moment he stood, his hand resting against the soiled baked bean cans, and thanked her. Calm settled through him at how right their union had been. He knew now. He knew that she loved him. He sat on the ground, his hand still in the box and leant his head against her bottom shelves. There was no need to clean up. He would sleep here tonight.

The moon had cracked a nasty smile in the night sky. The garden gates had clanged out a deranged melody in the wind. His mother had made him put the broom in the bin out in the back lane. She had refused to touch it herself. He had cried, sobs that were thick with humiliation. His mother had only pulled her dressing gown tighter around her in the cold wind that ripped through the night. She did not look at him, or even at the bin.

The wet patch of his pyjama pants had stuck cold against his thigh and Jimmy had known he was in the wrong. He felt keenly the injustice that his friend should have to pay for his own crime. That they should part on these terms. But he had known his mother was just trying to protect Broomie from him, and he could not blame her for that.

Saturdays
2003

The wheelbarrow is full of candlesticks and old clock radios. Tim has recently learnt that this is one of George's marketing tactics.

'Throw in something unexpected. They think they're looking for a new microwave, and then bam! They find a full set of cutlery inside and they realise that's really what they've needed all along. Got to make sure you keep the power off if you're going to store metal things in the microwave, though. You never know what kind of idiot presses some buttons on the thing without asking first.'

Tim picks up his tenth candlestick of the day and begins to half-heartedly polish the silver.

He'd really like to own his own store one day, and he'd hoped working for George would be good experience. George was a slick businessman who had made his fortune after starting from nothing. The rumours about his dealings with some of the underbelly of Sydney raised him even higher in Tim's estimation. The dark blue business suits, the confident gait, the way he cracked his knuckles – these were all things that Tim aspired to. But this, this polishing of candlesticks was not what he'd envisaged when he'd boasted to his friends that he'd be working for George Swan.

Tim looks up when the front door buzzer goes off and can't believe his luck to see the girl from the other week walk in, all casual. Tim plays it cool, pretending not to notice her. He's hoping to catch her in the act this time, then he can present her to George and then maybe he'll get some respect around here. No more polishing candlesticks.

She moves around the store slowly, picking up items and considering them from all angles before putting them down. She turns away from him and bends down to pick up something from the floor and Tim remembers how she got away from him the last time. That sweet bum walking out the door.

She notices him checking her out and he flushes with anger at being caught out, when really she's the one whose being caught. She turns her back on him and saunters to the counter up the back moving slowly toward the cash register. Tim creeps silently behind her, and he's just about to wrestle her to the ground, when George appears from the back room with his suitcase and strides straight past them both to the front door.

'This is my daughter, Tim. She's in charge for the rest of the afternoon. Make sure you finish those candlesticks!'

The door slams behind him before Tim can reply. Little bitch.

***

Ella reckons Saturdays are for fun family shopping in brightly lit shopping centres where sales assistants have orgasms when you pass them your credit card to pay for a plasma television.

Cash Palace is always quiet on a Saturday. It was more of a weekday place, for when the weirdos shop. And, besides, her dad is deadset against credit cards, and maybe orgasming too.

Ella stays behind the counter, flicking through the receipt book. She applies a careful smear of red lipstick, but Tim seems to be ignoring her now. A silence yawns between them, and Ella begins to realise she hasn't really thought beyond this point. Her grand-entrance glow is dwindling.

'So, how are you finding working for my dad?'

Tim looks back to the candlesticks. Through gritted teeth he manages, 'Yeah. Good. I suppose.'

She stares harder at the receipt book, looking for some kind of inspiration.

Ella had been hoping for fireworks. A brilliant bang-crash-smashing reaction from Tim. She can feel it in him, a fierce little animal that would tear her down given half the chance. She looks for the words to draw it out. Confrontation is where she shines.

'You don't have to keep doing that, you know.'

Tim glares at her now. 'You. Are. Not. My. Boss.'

He polishes harder, his face defiant, but her bright red lips split into an unexpectedly kind smile and the tension falls slack between them. She looks away.

'I know.' She smiles again, cocky. 'Let's go for lunch. It's dead here.'

'Maybe.'

Ella notices that he is careful in his response not to give her the authority he's just hotly denied. She likes that.

'I know an interesting place.' She opens the cash register and takes five dollars. She has been planning on paying Jimmy back anyway.

'Come on.' She slips her hand into his and drags him out, locking the door one-handed behind them. The manoeuvre is awkward, Tim offering nothing but the slack weight of his arm. But she feels victorious all the same.

Outside, rubber wheels rumble along the black tar in a blur; planes screech out above them. Noise pours into their bodies from every direction, silencing any possible conversation. His hand, now sweaty, stays folded in hers.

Ella leads him coyly through the rubbery welcome of the milk bar doorway. She wants to share her discovery. Jimmy is fiddling with the aerial of a radio. Today he seems peaceful, as if enjoying the humdrum of married life; the radio chatters away like a small child in the background. She elbows Tim to see if he's noticed. Tim raises his eyebrows and shrugs.

'What is this shit hole?' he asks.

'Do you want a milkshake?'

'Not really.'

'I'm getting one.'

'All right.'

'Two milkshakes please.' She hands Jimmy the five-dollar note eagerly. 'Keep the change.'

Jimmy frowns. Maybe he doesn't remember?

'I was here last week. I didn't have enough—'

'I know who you are.'

It seems he is unimpressed with her either way. He turns his back to make the milkshakes.

Well, whatever. She slumps into the booth next to Tim, suddenly at a loss why she's even come back here. Tim is looking up at the faded orange lampshades with no light bulbs inside and cracking his knuckles slowly. She risks a mean look in Jimmy's direction, and notices something odd about the way he is wiping down the counter. Pressing both palms flat, he moves them in slow rhythmical circles. As if he is stroking a stomach.

'Isn't this the place your dad's trying to buy?' Tim says.

'Huh?'

'This place. Your dad was talking about buying it the other day. I guess you could do it up pretty nice if you wanted. But it's pretty rank.'

'What? Nah. Dad wants the land, not the place. He'd like to see it smashed to the ground so he can make his mint.'

Tim nods knowingly. But Ella ignores him. She can't tear her eyes away from the old man.

'Just look at him,' she whispers.

'What?'

'You know … what he's doing.'

Tim glances over. 'I bet he doesn't even make milkshakes, you know. My uncle always said this place was just a drug front.' He cracks another knuckle and starts to kick at the wooden board under the chair opposite. Jimmy winces. Ella can't stand it.

'Fuck it. Let's go. Dad would be pissed if he knew we'd left anyway.'

Outside the store, she presses herself up close and kisses Tim hard to wipe out the confusion of the circles on the counter. He responds, his wiry body strangely powerful against hers, all bones and twitching muscles. His sweaty hands move up quickly under her shirt. He's in charge now.

Secrets crackle and spark between the buildings beside them.

The Willing Cuckold
1974

In the morning the milk bar was divided in two. The back wrapped in the purples and blues of morning bed-sheet shadows that begged Jimmy to linger a little longer. The front awash in the bright sunlight of the outside world, stubbornly shining in on them.

Jimmy paused at the precipice, reluctant to leave the groggy intimacy of the lover's dawn behind him, but resigned to the figure of his mother waiting at the front door.

Anthea leant heavily on the counter as she entered and Jimmy wondered if it was not time to buy her a walking stick. She had aged so much these two years since his father had died. Just after his death she had seemed infinitely lighter, her sharp face softened with grief. But as time wore on the familiar hardness had returned to her body, rendering her small frame more brittle than ever.

'Opening the store again today?' She sat slowly into one of the chairs, and wiped at her face with a handkerchief. 'This heat at this hour, it's too much.'

'Paul prefers the nightshift.'

'I'm sure he does.' She raised her eyebrows.

'He's busy during the day at the moment. Looking for houses.'

'I'm sure he is. Though I can't think why.'

'You know why, Ma.'

'Yes, I suppose I do.'

Jimmy rummaged through the top drawer behind the counter. 'Do you need some help with your shopping today?'

'Can't a mother just spend some time with her son?'

'Sure.'

They lapsed into silence. Jimmy began to stack the shelves behind him with clean glasses.

'He was always so much like your father.'

Jimmy had sensed this was where the conversation would go this morning.

'Not like you. You're more like me. I always did think you were a girl when I was pregnant.'

Jimmy was finding it hard to focus on his

mother's conversation. He could hear the soft banging of the open storeroom door against the wall. She was begging him to return. He spun, switched off the storeroom light and closed the door firmly. It was perhaps too stern a scolding for a little harmless flirting but he could not be like this with her in front of his mother. However, Anthea was far too focused on her other son's choice of partner to discern the subtle machinations of Jimmy's own love affair.

'It seems an odd choice to me. Don't you think?' she asked him.

'I don't know.'

'Of course you do. You know Fi better than any of us.'

'Do I?'

'Out of the blue, don't you think? It makes you wonder. They're in a big enough hurry to get the neighbours talking. Maybe you should have a talk with him.' She leant in and left her hand lightly on his arm. Her breath was garlicky.

'Ma, as if Paul gives a rat's what I think.'

Jimmy sighed heavily and drew his arm away from her. What did he care these days anyway? Fi and him were ancient history. In fact, they were more than that. What did he care if Paul wanted to get old-fashioned now? They seemed happy enough and it would probably give Jimmy more time alone with the store.

Well, almost alone. Lunchtime at the store

was always busier than he liked.

'Can I have two chocolate milkshakes please, one with extra chocolate. Do you mind if we eat our pies in here?' The man licked his lips. A pregnant woman was flicking through a magazine at the front while her two children clambered underneath the tables and chairs. A young couple was in the front booth, surrounded by textbooks and paper. The boy's thin face wore a practised expression of studious concentration. They had ordered one milkshake between them and sucked at the single straw in quick succession, eager to place their lips where the other's wet tongue had just been.

The man banged his coins onto the counter. Lately, inside the store all Jimmy could hear was money. The muffled tinkle inside the soft leather of ladies' purses. The reluctant slither of paper notes between sweaty fingers. Coins that scuttled and scraped hurriedly across the counter.

Everything had a price. Maybe even him. Maybe even love? Did she love them, these customers, the way she loved him? Sometimes it was hard to know. Men came in with the jangle of silver in their step and he was obliged to let them spend time with her. She did not seem to care. Perhaps, she even liked it. And was he so different from any other person that walked within her walls? Was he really any different from his brother who also opened and closed her cash register with such delight?

Jimmy hated watching Paul serve customers, stirring milkshakes, wiping the bench, grabbing the cigarettes from the shelf behind. Slosh. Wipe. Grab. Slam. His long arms moved fluidly; he knew that space as well as anyone, certainly as well as Jimmy. Paul's movements were authoritative, automatic and careless. He dropped things and laughed with customers about it. Did she like that? Jimmy sometimes attempted to recreate his brother's easy manner but his arms were too thin, his facial expression solemn, his actions too deliberate. He placed, he stroked, he tenderly clicked shut the cash register.

Jimmy stared at the coins on the counter in front of him, unable to reach out and take them. The two men with pies had sat in the booth at the very back of the store. They took up the whole booth between them.

Jimmy guessed they were working in the furniture factory down on Trafalgar Street. Sawdust floated from their hair and landed on the fresh pink upholstery. The mud from their shoes left dark smears against the legs of the table where they rested their feet. Jimmy flinched as the man on the right who had ordered the milkshakes brushed the sawdust from the seat onto the floor with his callused hand. The ginger hairs on his forearm were thick and curly.

Jimmy made the milkshakes hastily, forgetting to add the extra chocolate and only mixing them for half the usual time. Unable to take his eyes off the two men, he spilt milk all over the counter. How at ease they seemed with her. How quickly they made her their own. Marking her, using her, relaxing into the soft crimson of her seats.

Jealousy prickled at the back of his throat. The ginger-haired man dropped tomato sauce onto the tabletop as he lifted his pie up to his mouth. Jimmy felt sick as he watched the fat, greasy index finger stroke against her tabletop to retrieve the sauce. The man licked his fingers with gusto. He was slouched comfortably while he ate, cradled by her booth, as if he was having breakfast in bed.

Jimmy's face burned. Paul should have been here by now. Thursday lunch shift was his responsibility. Jimmy's vision filled with the moving limbs of the customers as they pressed and leant their flesh against her walls, her floors, her tables and chairs. Where was she? He stood within her yet she was elsewhere – caught up in her role-play with these others, with these strangers. How could she let them touch her like that? How could he?

He dialled Fi's number into the phone beside the sink. It rang out. The men were watching him now, probably wondering about their undelivered milkshakes. The pregnant woman continued to flick through the magazine, oblivious to her children banging their heads under the tables. Jimmy splashed some water on his face to dispel his growing nausea and moved toward their corner. His reluctant footsteps toward their table stomped upon his own heart.

Up until now he had been uncertain. There had been hints, the tinkling, the clattering, the swish and rustle of this painful reality but he had not wanted to hear them. He had tried to drown them out with faltering certainty that he was imagining it all. But this was just one in a series of humiliations he had experienced lately. He wasn't sure if he was embarrassed for her, so unashamedly soliciting money for affection and attention, or for himself, the willing cuckold who put the money in his own pocket. His ham-fisted heart broke between the smile of her doorway and the slam of her cash drawer.

He could not love a whore.

Placing the milkshakes on the table he saw the white and red straws leaning in towards each other, as if about to kiss. The mirroring of their paper cylinders stirred a yearning within him before the two men grabbed automatically for their long-awaited drinks, wrenching the straws apart. Thin lips guzzled the milk. Jimmy looked away and tried hard not to think about where Paul might be.

Making A Profit
1975

Jimmy's punch had been poorly thrown. George rubbed his cheek.

'I was just saying. Jesus Christ, Jimmy.'

'You take it back.'

'I don't understand, mate. Take what back?'

'What you said. What you said about this place ...' Jimmy looked away, and his voice sank to a mutter. 'What you said about *her*.'

Jimmy scanned the room darkly. Here they all were, another party, another night of sharing her with everybody, another night watching her lap up their affection. The thrust and slide of bodies against her seats and walls, the alcohol-infused sweat and skin left behind for him to clean her up in the early hours of the morning.

She would not give it up, her role of hostess. It was who she was. It was what she was built for. It was excruciating. But he understood her. She needed him. He squeezed his right hand, wondering if he should get some ice from the freezer.

'Yeah, I know – my face is harder than it looks, eh?' George winked at him. His round cheeks were flushed from the drink, his words a little slurred. 'Anyway, it's like I was saying. You could make a bloody mint with this place if you just did it up right. Now that it belongs to you and Paul outright, you could change it up, turn her into something more high-class, start actually selling alcohol here. I know some people. I could look into a license for you guys. You'll be family soon. It's the least I could do.'

'We're not interested.'

'So you say.' George winked again. Jimmy clenched his jaw. He'd always hated George with his smarmy winks and fat face. It had been George's idea to make people pay at the door tonight.

It seemed George was back for good this time. Back for good and hoping to go into business with Paul. George was even offering to buy into the milk bar. Probably he'd use the money he made tonight on the door. Probably he'd been pulling shit like this all over the country just to save enough money to come back and take her away from him.

Jimmy stormed away to the back kitchen. Out there he opened the freezer to find some ice for his hand. The room was spinning and he paused, unsure if he was about to vomit or not. Cold hands clasped over his eyes.

'Guess who?'

He turned to find Fi standing in front of him, her concern concealed behind a nervous smile. She must have seen him punch George. He held up his hand, which was beginning to look a little bruised and swollen.

Gently she took his hand in hers, turning it over and kissed it lightly. 'There you go, all better.'

They looked at each other a long time. She seemed to expect him to kiss her or something.

'I was just getting some ice for the swelling,' he said finally.

He turned to the freezer and rummaged around, looking for something that he could hold against his hand; finally; he settled on a bag of frozen peas. He leant against the freezer to steady himself. The room continued to spin. He felt disoriented and alone. He hated her when she was like this, taking whatever she could get. He wondered, did he really mean so much to her? She took him for granted.

Jimmy turned back. Fi was gone.

He needed another drink. He stumbled toward the fridge behind the counter filled with wine and beer. He opened the fridge wide and pulled out bottle after bottle of alcohol, slamming them down on the counter. Paul was watching him now too. They'd all been keeping such close watch on him since Mama had died. As if that was the problem.

Fi moved to join him on the other side of the counter. He ignored her and continued stacking.

'Jimmy?'

He did not respond.

'*Jimmy*?' She touched his wrist as he put down a bottle in front of her. He looked at her, furious and cold.

He opened one of the bottles with a pop, and began to fill up a milkshake glass with white wine. His movements were clumsy and the wine sloshed onto her dress.

'Shit, Jimmy. Get me something to clean up.'

He shrugged and took a swig straight from the bottle.

'You gonna pay for that, Jim?' Paul's arm wrapped proprietarily around Fi's waist.

'Are *you*?' Jimmy took another gulp of the wine.

'Well, you're the one drinking it.'

'So?'

'So, you know what we decided tonight. We're going to make a bit of a profit out of the party for once.'

'You decided.'

'Yeah, me and George. *We* decided, Jim. So are you going to pay for that bottle of wine?'

'I don't see why I should. I don't see why we've always got to sell stuff here.'

'Because we're a shop, Jimmy. Because we need to make money. Because we're a shop! Because that's how it bloody works!'

'Yeah, and it's bullshit. Dad didn't like it and neither do I.'

'What are you talking about? Dad loved this place.'

Jimmy kicked hard at the cupboard in front of him, and wiped his streaming nose.

'Yeah. Everybody loves this place.' Jimmy spat. 'It's disgusting.' He spun around. 'You disgust me!'

He turned the wine bottle on its head, pouring it all over the counter and onto the ground. Cheap booze for a cheap whore. They could have her. Fi, Paul, George. They deserved each other. He'd tried to make it work, but how could he? She was stubborn. She wouldn't listen. Maybe in the end he was just a replacement for his father. She'd see. He'd leave, then what would she do? She couldn't follow. Yes. She was powerless, stuck here in the ground. Stuck here with her customers, and her money and the exhaust fumes from the cars that streaked past her.

And why should he pay now? He'd never paid before.

He could not look at her. He shut his eyes. But he was too drunk, he needed to lean against her bench for support. With satisfaction he felt her pain at his revulsion. He opened his eyes again and smashed the wine bottle to the ground.

'You clean up, Paul.' Jimmy stalked out through the crowd of people. Reaching the door he did not linger as he usually would to touch her handle, but stormed through and slammed the glass behind him. He heard it crack, but did not turn. Instead he stumbled on into the night, away from her. Away from them all.

He knew he needed to leave, to end this sick fantasy. He looked back up the street, she was barely visible, an orange dot that blurred as he blinked. No. She would not follow him.

He would be free.

A Seamstress of Necessity
2003

'Can you make me something, Aunty Fi?'

'Like what?' Aunty Fi does not look up from her sewing.

'A tablecloth.' Ella has been thinking about a gift for Jimmy. Something to show him that she understands.

'A tablecloth? Why on Earth would you want a tablecloth?'

'I dunno. I just do. Does it matter really?' Ella picks up a half-finished dress from one of the huge piles of fabric strewn across the couch and holds it up against her. She can't imagine being that fat.

'So, a tablecloth?' Fi knows better than to push the point.

'Yeah. So. Can you make something like that or not?'

'That depends. Is it for your room?'

'No, nothing like that.'

'What's brought this on?'

'Oh I don't know. You wouldn't understand.' Ella slips the huge dress on and gets her head stuck in one of the sleeves. Face hidden, she asks, 'You know Jimmy Panagakos, from down the road?'

Aunty Fi's hands tighten on the fabric as she runs it under the needle.

Ella tries again, louder. 'Aunty. You know Jimmy from down the road?'

Fi stops sewing, and folds her arms across her chest. She had smiled too eagerly when Jimmy came back. She had sat underneath the jacaranda tree in their old back garden and smiled with her whole body at the sight of him. His awkward frame in one of his father's old suits leaning against the back fence in the grey glare of that cloudy day after Paul's funeral. It had been such a sweet relief after everything that had happened to see his face again, fragile, dark and waiting. She had gripped his familiar arm tight in the church earlier that day for comfort amongst the sea of uncertainty that faced her now. His skinny arm, cold and pale against her hot hand – the only solid thing left for her.

She had spun her wedding ring around her finger while she watched him. Paul's ring. Her finger was sweaty and constricted underneath it. Jimmy had seemed distracted, far away, intent on not looking in her direction. She had put the ring in her pocket and stood up.

'We're so glad you came back, Jim. We weren't sure if you would—'

He had looked into her face, as if only just noticing that she had been there in the garden with him that whole time. His look had split her open wide. He knew her. He had always known her best. There had been hope for her, in amongst all that mess.

She had approached him clumsily, her high heels sinking and sticking in the grass. She stepped out of them and stood barefoot beside him, leaning against the fence, her breasts against his arm.

'I'm so glad you're back, Jimmy. Back for good now?'

'Yes.'

'I'm so glad. Did I say that?'

'Yes.' A smile flickered across his face, and then he frowned. 'I'm going to keep the milk bar.'

'Oh good. George will be pleased. Him and Paul were going to—'

Jimmy moved away from her abruptly and sat down on the back step. She followed him, resting her hand on his knee.

'Okay, I understand how you feel about my brother. I guess what I mean is … I'll help you. I can help you with the store.'

'You can't help me, Fi.' Jimmy moved her hand off his leg. She flushed, exposed.

'But you'll need help, Jimmy.'

'I just want it to be the two of us.'

'Oh, me too,' she said. 'So much. I've been so stupid, Jimmy. We've been so stupid. It can just be you and me; George doesn't have to be involved at all.' She wanted to tell him about the pregnancy then; it seemed right that he would be the first person to know. She paused looking for the right way to share her news, and leant in again so they were sat shoulder-to-shoulder, just like they used to when they had to eat their ice creams outside as kids.

'Just me and her. Alone.'

She frowned, confused. 'You've met somebody?'

'No, I've come back for the milk bar. I only came back for her.'

The soft chanting of the sewing machine brings Fi back into the room with Ella. The gnawing of the needle into the soft material is strangely reassuring. She punctures old dreams and hides her secrets in the hems. Jimmy's choice still nibbles at her flesh in tiny mouthfuls that tickle and sting, leaving her tattered around the edges. Her clothes struggle to hold their fibres together, unravelling around fingers and catching on splinters in doorframes.

She is a seamstress, not by choice but of necessity.

The old Singer is warm to touch after it has been running for a while. They move together, old friends. Her comfort and her final retreat, she can hide nothing from her Singer.

Ella has found the neck hole in the dress and Fi realises that she is still waiting for an answer. Fi considers her words carefully.

'Yes. I know of Jimmy Panagakos.'

'So you don't know him then?'

'Not really.'

'Oh.'

Fi senses that she is losing her rare audience with Ella. 'He's just a sad old man, Ella.'

'Yeah, but he's a bit interesting, don't you think?'

'What do you mean? He's just old.' Fi's heart races.

'Nothing.'

Jimmy had not chosen her. And could she blame him? Fi slides another piece of material through her sewing machine. She feels the puncture of the needle all over her body. It's predictable munching stitches the unravelling threads of her life back together.

She had been directionless really without Paul, without Jimmy.

It had seemed a small thing at the time, to leave the child behind. In the end she had trusted George more than herself, and certainly more than Jimmy.

The morning they'd taken her away was when the unravelling really began. They'd picked her up off the streets, nearly naked because her clothes just kept unstitching.

Fi slides her finger carefully under the needle of the Singer. Her relief is immediate, as the blood seeps from her body into the fabric beneath. Ella cries out as if it is her own finger.

'Bloody hell Aunty Fi, are you alright?' she asks.

But Fi does not know how to answer.

A Museum Exhibit
2003

George's nervous animal stench seeped through the air-conditioned room, undermining the professional nature of his carefully crafted presentation to the local council.

'And in this slide, you might observe the serious structural damage to this building, which again, shows the danger it poses to the general public. Councillors, these buildings are taking up valuable retail space which could be used more profitably that would greatly benefit the local area.'

He clicked to his next slide, the mouldy awning of the shop next to his own. Clicked again to the next slide showing the broken windows of the old laundry shop.

The boredom in the room was palpable.

George clicked to another slide.

'Here you can observe the termite—'

'Mr Swan,' one of the younger men at the table interrupts him, 'we are very busy, and were told that you would be presenting us with an overall plan for the renewal of Parramatta Road. But from what we have seen this evening, your proposal is not appropriate to this forum. You must go through the appropriate development application processes. Frankly, though, the viability of traditional retail precincts along the road has been questionable for many years.'

George clicked to his final slide – the one he had been unsure about including. His own face, thirty-five years younger, smiles out proudly under the brightly lettered awning of the milk bar. Fi and Paul stand next to him. They are holding a document between the three of them. Something that Paul had written up to make his part in the business official. The key document that went missing after Paul died was what his case for the milk bar relied on. Well, that and Fi's half share of the business.

'Now this slide is from 1975. That's me on the left with my business partner Paul Panagakos and his wife, my sister, Fiona. We were running the place together, and though you can't make out the writing on the document between us, it said—'

For the first time that evening the councillors are actually looking properly at his slide. A younger woman towards the front piped up before he could finish making his point.

'Wow, that's amazing – 1977, you reckon? The milk bar looks exactly the same. It hasn't changed a bit. That's just incredible! Have you got more shots like this? We could put on an exhibition at the library or something.'

'Yeah I've always wanted to go into that place. Have you ever been in there?'

'I hear the milkshakes are still two dollars.'

'I went in there once when I was a kid. Remember when the movie cinema was still down the road?'

General murmuring of wonder spread through the room. George could feel himself losing his already tenuous grip on the group. He cleared his throat.

'Well, no disrespect, lady, but it has changed a lot. It's not the same building, its nothing like it was, it's a fucking useless shell of a thing that is falling apart!'

An uncomfortable silence descended on the room. The air conditioner rumbled on mechanically.

'What I mean is,' George pushed on carefully, 'it's no longer viable as a business. Jimmy

Panagakos doesn't want to sell anything. Quite frankly, he shouldn't even be allowed in there at all. It's a blight on the whole strip. It's not some heritage-listed piece of wank that'll bring back the glory days of Parramatta Road. I'm telling you, the best thing we can do for the building and for Mr Panagakos is to knock the damn thing down.'

'And that is your proposal then?' the young man from earlier asked him.

'Yes. Knock it down. Build something better, something that has a function.'

'As I said earlier, Mr Swan, this just isn't the correct forum for your proposal. Thank you. Now, to the next item on the agenda, the community garden on Charles Street.'

George leaned into the sweaty palm of the humid summer night and felt it wrap its grubby fingers round him. Fucking pinko bastards and their love for grit and grime and so-called history. Fucking Jimmy and that fucking perverted milk bar bullshit. George began the short walk home, thinking about his next move.

***

Fi glanced up from her sewing to find George standing in the doorway, a badly concealed look of desperation on his sweaty face. He smiled at her and her stomach tightened in apprehension of the conversation she knew was coming.

'How was the meeting?'

'Pointless.' The smile slid from his face and he cautiously stepped toward the pile of scrap fabric in the corner of the room. He picked up a flimsy scrap of purple lycra and searched the sad bulk of the woman in front of him for some trace of the young spark of beauty she had been before the whole sorry business began, before Jimmy betrayed them all. 'You need to sell me your half of the milk bar.'

'You know I can't do that, George.'

'Of course you can. I'd give you a good price. You could take a holiday away from here. Make something of your life. It's what Paul would have wanted for you, for us both.'

'You don't know what Paul wanted.'

George threw the scrap onto the ground in disgust. 'I know a damn sight better than you what Paul wanted for that place, Fi. What Paul and me dreamt of together. I was his friend. You were just—'

'I was his wife, George.'

'We knew everything about each other. Everything.'

'I can't sell it.'

'Why?'

'You know why.'

'I want you to say it.' George stepped towards her now, his hands fisted around his own private rage.

Fi turned back to the sewing machine avoiding his pleading eyes.

'Everyone knew you were in love with Jimmy, Fi.'

'It's not mine to sell, George.' Her chin was trembling.

'You're a fucking embarrassment. Pull yourself together. Fuck that idiot. We owe him nothing.'

'He loved me.'

'All he loves is that fucking shop.'

She began to sob into her hands. The lycra around rolls of her fat shimmered under the light. Disgust seared through him. He pulled the folded power of attorney document slowly from his pocket.

'This doesn't have to be your problem anymore, Fi. Just let me take care of things. Let me take care of you.'

She turned her wet face toward him and looked at the document. She thought of all the rocks she'd thrown through the milk bar's front window, of Jimmy sitting inside, refusing to come out and face her.

'I don't need you to take care of me, George.'

'Then, it's time to tell Ella.'

'George, you can't be serious. It would ruin her.'

'She's almost 18. She deserves to know. She should have a say in its future.'

'She's not going to want to knock it down, George.'

'As if she gives a shit about that store! You just want to protect yourself. You can't bear it, can you now? What you did to us.'

'You will lose her, George. We will lose her.'

Uprooted
2003

Ella is cleaning out the old filing cabinet in the office out the back of Cash Palace. Less of an office and more of a hallway really. When she was a kid she called this room 'the in-between', because it wasn't really the store and it wasn't really home either. It has two doors – one that opens into Cash Palace and is disguised in the back wall of the store as a mirror. George has always had dreams of one day turning this door into a proper two-way mirror that he can use to spy on people. The other door at the back of the in-between opens into their kitchen, a dank little room complete with sky blue linoleum and a small window that offers a spectacular view of next door's brick wall.

No windows in the in-between though. A dusty naked light bulb hangs above her dad's desk, lighting up the various photocopies of old floor plans and her father's wild scrawl on various post-it notes stuck on the underside of the staircase that makes up half the ceiling.

She's not sure exactly what she's supposed to be clearing out of the filing cabinet. 'Just get rid of any of the old crap in there – you know, anything older than ten years can go,' George had said. Seemed more to her that he just wanted her out of the way.

Her fingertips already feel thick with the grime of dusty receipts and letters and she's sneezing about ten times a minute. Fucking George. She's been at it for half an hour when she gets to the back of the second drawer and finds a file with her name on it.

She pulls it out and sits down on the floor with her back against the cold metal of the filing cabinet. Inside she finds her old school reports, some scribbly kid drawings, and a photo she has never seen before.

It is a picture of George standing next to some pregnant woman who is scowling at the camera. They are standing in front of an old butcher shop. The awning above the shop says, *O'Dwyer's Meats*.

Ella knows the building well, but not as a

butcher's. A corner spot. Prime position. Just a block down from *Cash Palace*. Ella knows it as the powder-puff building, its bright pink paint long faded and peeling. It's awning now reads *Ligne Noir Paris* in curly black writing. When she was younger Ella had imagined exotic, worldly ladies visiting the store for their makeup and accessories. She'd spent many hours at its cloudy windows coveting the fake alligator handbags. Ella couldn't ever remember that place being open. But it still looked the same as when she was a kid, as if it had closed just the day before as normal. The 'Open' sign still lying on the counter waiting to grace the door once more. Only the thick layer of dust across everything and the pile of mouldy newspapers and old utility bills at the doorstep gave it away.

Ella's mind reels.

George had always told her that her mother lived far away and had been too young to keep her. But Ella had built her own more detailed story from other tales her father told. Like the years he'd spent working on the trains, travelling from town to town across Australia. Seen more of this country than most, he reckoned, been to some remote places, witnessed some strange things, lived a life. He'd say, 'Believe me, most of it's just scrub and weeds and desert. We've got something here; this place could really be somewhere.'

As opposed to the nowhere you pass through on your way to getting somewhere else, is what she'd guessed he meant.

She sits staring at the photo for a long time. The fantasy mother of her dreams still more real to her than this scowling half-shadow.

A sick resignation permeates her body at the truth of who she is and where she belongs. To the road. Not just born on it, but a product of it. Another thing left behind, like the pink powder-puff building, to raise the occasional eyebrow but in general to elicit shrugged shoulders and indifference.

The nausea overwhelms her and she crawls from the in-between into the kitchen and towards the sink. She feels groundless, each stumble forward like an endless falling into the wide-open sky of the dirty blue linoleum beneath her. So she doesn't notice at first, Fi standing on the stairs, watching her. When she reaches the sink she pulls herself to standing and waits for the building wave of vomit to descend. Slowly, though, she feels the coolness of the floor beneath her feet again and the wave within in her subsides to a bubbling heat in her belly. Hearing the familiar creak of Fi on the stairs behind her she runs out the back door into the pouring rain of the afternoon storm.

As her running slows to a walk she wonders where she is going. More than ever, Ella craves a destination. She wants to get the fuck out of her current life but can think of no one she knows who offers a real alternative to the eat-sleep-shit-consume-die equation that she has witnessed since Year Dot. Maybe that's why Jimmy and his milk bar stirs something in her.

The storm has denuded the branches of a jacaranda tree, the back lane a soggy, purple carpet of broken petals. She rubs the ball of her foot into the petals and watches with despair how quickly purple can turn to brown. Her own heart feels both naked and squashed.

The roads play at rivers as the water seeks out ancient routes tarred over. People trundle past her without a second glance in their grey city uniforms. Under their umbrellas they wear a grimace of determination as they surge forward in the wet evening wind. Only the small damp patches at their knees suggest a hint of something else, a snatch of vulnerability in the mechanical march homeward. One man smiles at her manically, suit soaked through, apparently full of glee at being caught out by Mother Nature.

Was it such a radical thing, to expose yourself willingly to the falling rain?

She finds herself instead at the counter of Jimmy's Milk Bar. Its pink-and-white marbled surface bears a striking resemblance to raw meat. Her stomach turns uncomfortably as she traces the white swirls. Jimmy must be out the back.

Was there a bell she could ring to let him know she was here? Would he care?

She couldn't explain the growing sense of recognition inside her, the odd affinity she felt with the decaying building which kept drawing her back. Just that it felt subversive and stubborn. It wasn't trying to sell her something; it just was.

Jimmy appears in the kitchen doorway, broom in hand. He must have been sweeping out back. She can't figure that out either, how he's always cleaning and how the place never feels clean. Not in that spick-and-span way you see in ads on TV. But maybe it's just the lighting, or lack thereof.

'Did George send you?'

'No.'

'Who, then … Fi-ona?'

The name fell oddly out of his mouth, a kind of accidental prayer laden with foreboding. Ella raised an eyebrow sceptically. 'Aunty Fi?'

'You're George's daughter.' He says her father's name like a swearword.

'Yeah, well. So what? I don't like him either.'

Jimmy nods his head slowly, taking this in. 'So, why are you here then …?'

'Ella. My name is Ella.'

'Why are you here, Ella?'

She stares at him, contemplating this unanswerable question. Ella turns her gaze to the floor uneasily, not wanting to break the silence and unable to justify her presence there.

'Can I have a chocolate milkshake?'

Jimmy nods slowly, and turns to the freezer to pull out the milk.

'Froths better when it's almost frozen,' he explains conversationally, kindly even.

She wonders what other odd bits of milk bar wisdom he might deign to share with her if she sticks around long enough. He hands her the milkshake, and she puts two dollars down on the counter in front of him before he can ask, and goes to sit down in one of the booths facing out to the street. Peak-hour buses pull up in front of the store every couple of minutes; their brakes sighing out into the night. Commuters pour out from their doors, teeth clenched against the rain. Everybody going somewhere else, criss-crossing her in every direction to get there. Only here inside the milk bar is there a kind of silence, a wholeness in the void of constant noise.

'I'm lonely,' she says suddenly, more to herself than to Jimmy. But the words hang in the air between them, held somehow by the mirrors and the old floorboards and the peeling of the ornate cornice of the ceiling. She feels heard in a way unfamiliar to her. It quivers through her body.

A familiar round silhouette fills the doorway of the milk bar, hesitant behind the rubber strips of the entrance. Finally, Aunty Fi parts the rainbow curtain wide enough to poke her head through and survey the scene. Her face wears its habitual look of caved-in defeat, but her usually frizzy hair is plastered down flat to her head from the rain. Her thoughts about finding Ella in this place are unreadable.

Ella had always wondered what had happened in Aunty Fi's life to render her facial expression in such a permanently downtrodden shape. It is as if someone has stepped directly onto her face, mashing her features together in a kind of disgruntled resignation. Ella realises all over again how little she really knows about Aunty Fi. What hopes hung dead from the corners of that mouth, pulling it down so decidedly? Which thoughts knitted her eyebrows together in that expression of permanent anxiety? What other fresh secrets lay hidden between the rolls of lycra-clad fat cascading down her body?

'I've been looking all over for you for hours! George told me, well he told me that…' Her voice trails off, unable to voice what has been silent between them for so many years. Her feet remain firmly planted outside of the milk bar itself, body awkwardly craning through the door to look at Ella.

'Well, here I am.'

'What are you doing in here?'

'What does it look like I'm doing?' Ella gestures to the metal milkshake cup, now almost empty. She knows she is being facetious, but she can't help herself.

'We've been worried sick about you.'

'Really?' Ella slurps on the dregs of her milkshake casually to indicate her disbelief.

'You know George. He hasn't said anything but—'

The colour drains from Fi's face. She leans in further to take in the rest of the store around Ella, her eyes locking with Jimmy's.

'Good evening. Would you like a milkshake?' he asks her, formally.

'No, thank you.' Her reply is equally stiff, face turning scarlet. With anger or embarrassment? It's hard for Ella to tell.

'I'll meet you at home, Aunty Fi. I'll be back in time for dinner.'

Fi needs no encouragement. She is backing away from the door before Ella has finished her sentence, her mouth opening and closing as if to say something more.

Ella is grateful to be left alone with Jimmy. Though Jimmy's expansive mood seems to have evaporated, his mouth forming a flat line across his face as he stares out the window at the traffic. Ella smiles at him and shrugs her shoulders in apology.

'I better get going too then. Thanks for … everything.' She walks up to the counter to pass over her milkshake cup, but it's as if she doesn't exist for him anymore. It's as if she doesn't exist for anyone. Panic spills through her and she brings the cup back to her chest and flees, running from the helplessness reflected in every mirror along the wall of that place, peeling from the ceiling in the sad little flakes to rest on the recently swept floor.

Reaching the road she slips out of her shoes and steps into the gutter, squatting down to fill the metal cup. The water is warm from the sun-baked concrete. It pools around her feet and splashes up into her face from the wheels of passing cars. She dreams of a river running before her, squints to imagine the telegraph poles are eucalypts filled with the cries of Currawongs as the day sky turns its bright face away from her own.

But then the streetlights blink on, beaming from the heads of those limbless tree trunks. She stands in the gutter a little while longer, another dead tree with no roots. Only cement holds her straight in the ground.

Attempted Rescue
2003

Ella splutters and burps up her beer. Tim laughs at her. He bangs her on the back, kisses her on the neck. He treats her body like an extension of his own. A long dormant sneer rises to her lips.

'Will you fuck off, Tim?' She burps again and he laughs. She starts laughing too, despite herself. She must be drunker than she thought. Tim pulls her back to lie down with him in the grass under the Hills Hoist. He avoids her look of irritation and stares up at the sky, his face assuming a far-off look; she can't pick if he's for real or putting it on.

'Your dad offered me a promotion today.'

The ground feels like it's rolling underneath her like the ocean and she struggles to her elbow to look him in the face.

'What?'

'A promotion.'

'To do what?'

'I dunno. I guess to have more of an input in the way the business is run. He sees potential in me. Wants to keep things in the family.'

'Tim, you're not in my family.'

'Yeah, but you know, I mean we're together and stuff. And this is big for me. This is one step closer.'

'One step closer to what?'

'Being in charge, making money.'

'Being in charge of what?'

'I dunno. Running my own place. I've got big plans, Ella. Big plans.'

Ella groans.

'George says he'll sell me one of his places at a discount one day, let me pay it off slowly. Then we'll have a place we can live together. You can get out of this house just like you're always saying you want to.'

'Some escape plan, Tim.'

Ella rolls away from him onto her back, and looks up at the wiry arms of the hills hoist spread out above them like a giant cage.

She's about to utter the words that have been circling in her head for weeks. That it's over, that she can't stand him, that she's leaving, when a waft of smoke hits her nostrils and bites into her lungs. It's thick, close and urgent. Something actually burning. Not just some far-off scrub on the outskirts of suburbia, but something more complex than wood and leaves and possum fur. It gnaws at her lungs, making her sick with dread. Or is it just too much beer?

She bolts through the house to the front of the store and then out onto the Parramatta Road. Tim is stumbling behind her, laughing.

'You're crazy! What are you doing now?'

'Can't you smell that?'

'What?'

'Something's burning. I thought it might have been—'

She has her face up against the window of the milk bar trying to see in, but there's nothing to see. The glass soothes her pulsing forehead. She leans into it, grateful for the comfort.

'You are wasted, man.'

She jolts back from the window, self-conscious.

'Am not.'

But Tim isn't looking at her anymore. He's standing in the gutter, head craned back, wide eyed with excitement.

'Fuck, you're right about something burning, though! Check it out!'

She joins him on the road and leans back

to try and see what he's looking at. Smoke is billowing from the windows at the top level of the milk bar. She staggers to keep her balance.

'Fuck. What should we do?' She runs back to the window, trying to see in again for any sign of Jimmy. The dark counter is desolate without his shadow behind it. She thinks she can hear the crackling and creaking of the fire upstairs, a kind of moaning.

'We need to break in.'

'Fuck no, are you serious? What for?'

'To rescue … to rescue …' She wants to say, *The building*. But she settles for, 'To rescue Jimmy.'

'Who?'

'You know, the old guy who runs the place.'

'Yeah right. He probably lit this shit up himself for insurance money. He'd make a lot more out of it that way than selling it or paying for someone to knock it down.'

'He wouldn't do that,' she says quietly.

They hear a loud crack and suddenly a burning beam crashes through the ceiling. Flames light up the inside of the store, brighter than Ella has ever seen it. The fire licks its way easily across the old wooden floor and up over her counter. Her smooth, vulnerable belly. Her body pops and crackles, vinyl melting black at the edges. The smoke is sweet with plastic and old chocolate. Ella hears the store screaming and she pictures Jimmy somewhere inside, refusing to leave her. Dying together. The wailing builds louder and louder, ringing in her ears, or is it sirens from approaching fire trucks? Pain reverberates through her body in waves, as the glass at her hands grows hot.

Tim grabs her round the middle and drags her to the other side of the road. She clutches at the air toward the store, not wanting to let go. She throws up smoky beer in the gutter. She keeps retching long after there is nothing left in her stomach. Tim stands to the side, sirens painting his awkward face red and blue.

Reunited
2003

The milk bar yawns its blackened mouth into the stale beginnings of a February morning. Fi did not move from the safety of her bed in the night when she heard the sirens, but the smell has drawn her out early.

The pavement is wet under her bare feet. She hardly ever comes out here. Every crack in the pavement speaks to her of another time. Of the little girl she was once, of the woman she became. She's not sure if she likes it – the way the old laundry is still there, *For Lease* sign in the window, of course, and graffiti scrawled along the white tiles of the doorway, but the tiny bench she used to sit on when she was waiting for Mama is still there. It seems almost magical the way the bench had not changed, the old thumbtack still stuck in the side that she used to fiddle with. How is it possible, that her flesh could swell and flow and sag beyond recognition, and that a humble meaningless bench held its form so well?

She used to wait on that bench long after the sheets had dried, her stockings getting caught on the splinters and laddering as she kicked her feet backward and forward. Mrs Wong behind her counter reading the paper would look up from time to time to give her looks of reproach and pity that were destined for her mother, and would be amplified tenfold when Mrs Swan did eventually reappear to 'pick up the sheets' with no extra tip for the free babysitting.

It was always better when Jimmy was there. He'd think of something fun to play. Imagining the washing machines were the engine of their space ship bound for the outer reaches of the galaxy. They would be explorers together; the dryer doors submarine windows, or magical portals to another universe.

Jimmy was often there, because he spent so much time with his dad at the milk bar next door. But no, it hadn't been a milk bar then, she has to remind herself. It seems such a long time since she and Jimmy ran circles round those boxes of fruit and veg in the sunshine.

It is a long time.

She recalls her reason for venturing out of the house today. Her nose taking in the faint smell of smoke still hanging in the air, and cranes her neck to inspect the full extent of the damage to the building she still thinks of as her own.

Black tears trickle from the dark sockets of the second-storey windows. She slips under the police tape at the front for a closer look. Somebody's left the front door open. Officers long gone.

Empty.

Deserted.

She kicks the twisted skeleton of one of the old chairs.

Who cares? Not her, not really. Gingerly, she opens the blackened metal door of the fridge behind the counter. There is a bottle of milk, almost full. She picks it up. Still cold. Weighty in her hand.

Her heart thumps hard. Is he still here? Is that him? That burnt pile of ash on the floor at her feet? Or over there in the curl of melted vinyl in the red booth seats? Did he stay till the end? Burned like a sacrifice on the funeral pier? Raised up and turned to stars in the night sky?

She imagines his constellation in the smoke stained ceiling that drips still with the fireman's water. His bones changed to charred wood, indistinguishable from the floor.

Fi looks around for him again, feeling stupid, hoping against hope he had the sense to make a run for it last night. But she is alone. She has been alone a long time.

She stands behind the counter, in Jimmy's well-worn spot. The damage is not as bad as it looks from outside. You could replace the old bench top, give the ceiling a lick of fresh paint. Maybe take the mirrors down.

Jimmy appears like a vision at the front door, leaning into a walking stick, a plastic hospital tag tied around his small wrist. He seems naked, without the cloak of the dark indoors around his body. She can hardly believe it, her relief. The way she still loves this man.

'Come in,' she says, gesturing expansively to their shared ruin.

Jimmy hobbles to one of the undamaged booths without looking at her and eases himself into the seat.

'Would you like a milkshake?' she asks him in an echo of his own question.

Jimmy is silent for a long time, his hands splayed across the table, his eyes shut. Finally, he turns to her and smiles warily.

'Yes. You can make me a milkshake.'

Fi moves quickly to the fridge, feeling watched, her body ablaze under his stare. She delivers his drink to the table and returns to her spot behind the counter, a place she's wanted to stand for so many years.

And so he lets her stands there. With the lights out, she moves her hands through the black charcoal in slow rhythmic circles. Outside, the bright morning traffic skirts past them all without a sideways glance.

Escape
2003

Ella waits behind the counter at Cash Palace, her morning shift almost over. Hardly anybody has been in today – always fewer people about when it's raining and the rain's been going all week. Her nervous hands look for things to fiddle with: the buttons on the cash register, the zipper of her backpack at her feet. She checks her wallet again to make sure the money and the bus ticket are still there.

The photo is on the counter in front of her. She flips it over in her hands distractedly, looking for further clues, some signal in the slope of the handwriting on the back, some message for her in their younger faces.

Nothing from this place would be coming with her. She would leave it all behind, like she'd been meaning to do forever. She hasn't been inside the milk bar since the fire. She's walked past a few times, but the doors are closed and it's not clear if Jimmy is inside or not. That final refuge has been stolen from her also. She wonders what will happen to Jimmy and his milk bar now. Perhaps George will have his victory. She doesn't know how she feels about that. She doesn't know how she feels about a lot of things now. The urgency to escape, pulling like a rip tide through her body, is the only certain thing in her life.

The buzzer goes off as George leans into the front door with his shoulder. He is carrying a large box. Sweaty and cheerful he sidles his way to the counter and, not seeing the photo puts the box down on top of it. Ella looks inside the box to see a small model town. On closer inspection she realises with horror that it is a miniature version of the road she knows so well, but with some alterations. Jimmy's Milk Bar is gone along with a lot of the other buildings in that block; there are trees and brightly painted apartment blocks with no backyards. There are only three or four cars placed just so on this fantasy road.

'So, what do you think?' he asks her expectantly.

Ella watches him closely, trying to take in this

new version of the man she had dismissed as her father all these years.

'It's interesting, I guess,' she offers.

'I thought maybe if the council could really *see* it, they'd begin to come around. You know, it's been so hard to get people to see this place differently. See it how it could be.'

Ella looks down at her stuffed backpack on the ground between her feet and back at George, and for the first time really reads the obsession written so indelibly across his face. She is momentarily thrown, but her desire for freedom has made her ruthless, and she lifts the box up to retrieve the photograph from underneath, throwing it down into the centre of the George's fantasy land.

George, delicately picks out the photograph from the model town, careful not to knock any of it over. His finger moves gently across the grey cardboard of the road in front of the huge apartment blocks.

'Fi, she owns half the milk bar you know,' he says, carefully.

'What? Jimmy's Milk Bar?'

'*Jimmy's* milk bar, yeah right,' George snorts. 'Fi and me were going to do great things with that building.'

Ella's knees give a little, and she leans into the counter to keep her standing.

'You'll see, Ella, everything is going to work out.'

She bends down and slings the heavy backpack over her shoulder and begins to walk towards the door.

'I hope it does, George.'

George moves towards her now, grabbing her arm. She prises his fingers from her sleeve.

'I'm sorry, George.'

She moves to the door and the buzzer screeches, calling out her departure to anyone who cares to hear it. Shutting the door behind her she sees George standing in the middle of the shop his head twisting back and forth between her and his prized model town on the counter. She walks away slowly, her heart fierce and breaking.

At the milk bar she pauses and rummages through her bag, pulling out the milkshake cup she stole last time she was there. She had been hoping to give it back. That the shop might open again before she left. She peers in through the closed front door and knocks against it just in case Jimmy is inside. She waits a minute, but nobody comes. She puts the milkshake cup back in her backpack.

Maybe just one thing from this place could come with her.

Return
1985

Jimmy fumbled with the key to the front door. He couldn't bear the idea that she might shrink back at his touch. Still, there was only one way to find out.

He slid the key in gently and turned the old lock. With a loud clunk, she welcomed him in. A film of dust had settled upon her bright surfaces between Paul's death and his own return. Jimmy eyed her disuse with an unexpected pleasure. Perhaps she had become more demure in his absence. He could barely contain his excitement at her obvious pleasure in seeing him; he looked instinctively to her storage cupboard, but chose instead to sit down in one of the booths.

He had spent ten long years trying to forget her. Ten years as a bricklayer in Adelaide hadn't cured him. Every new wall was a reminder of her painful absence. Every new building sang out to him for attention. But he could not have betrayed her.

He had irrationally longed for her to follow him, surprise him one day on a new corner in Adelaide. He had railed against the cruel twist of architectural requirement that left her rooted to the spot, entrenched and immovable. But wasn't that partly what he had loved about her? People were flighty, their roots buried abstractly in sentimental attachments, in unreliable memories.

Now, having returned he had no idea what to do next. He felt guilty, knowing that his own joy inside her walls was fundamentally connected with Paul's absence, Paul's death. As if his private longing to return had somehow propelled the stranger's car toward Paul. But like so many people had said at the funeral, just too much traffic on Parramatta Road these days.

He sat in the booth a long time, watching the light fade and the streetlights come on. How often had he thought about these simple moments in the last ten years? He left her front door open, but no one came in. There was no fresh milk in the fridge anyway. He sat on in the darkness at a complete loss.

Sometime late in the evening George's stocky silhouette in the kitchen doorway broke through Jimmy's quiet reverie. George looked embarrassed.

'Oh, you're here. I wasn't sure if the front door would still be open so I just let myself in through the back.' George sat down heavily on the seat opposite Jimmy. His face was drawn, his eyes red. Jimmy was taken aback. He had perhaps underestimated the genuine regard George had had for his brother.

'Yes, I'm here.'

'So what are you going to do with the place? Fi says you don't want our help.'

'No.'

'You should know your brother wouldn't have wanted that, Jim.'

'Paul's not here, is he?'

George's face darkened.

'No. I guess he's not.'

George drew in breath, as if about to say something and then stopped, thinking better of it. They sat opposite each other staring at the table.

'I'd like to do what's right, Jim. I'm happy to buy you out, but Fi says she'll only sell her half if you sell yours.'

A wave of gratitude swept through Jimmy at Fi's loyalty.

'I don't want to sell.'

'She said you'd say that. Thing is, mate, I think she's kind of hoping that you two might … I mean she'd never say it outright, Paul's only just gone and that. But you two were always close. You mean a lot to her.'

'Yeah, as Paul's replacement,' he scoffed.

'Don't be a dickhead, mate. I'm just saying you should think about it. No one wants to force anything on anyone. But you might change your mind, once you've had a chance to … settle back in.' George stood up abruptly and stuck his hand out. The walls bristled.

Jimmy stood slowly and took George's hand. 'I'm sorry for your loss, George.'

George snatched his hand back, bewildered and then furious. He stormed out through the front door. Jimmy walked slowly behind him and closed the door with relief. Softly, he traced the crack in the glass from his own exit years earlier, ashamed that he had scarred her permanently. Then he settled down in one of her booths to sleep, breathing in her familiar vinyl scent.

Hours later he was woken by the sound of glass smashing. Something had crashed through the front window. At first in a stupor he feared that a car had swerved into the store, but as he came to he saw half a brick lying on the floor, surrounded by broken glass. He ran to the front door and out onto the street, but whoever had thrown it was long gone.

In the silence of the night he inspected the ugly jagged hole in her beautiful face. He resolved to call the window repairman first thing tomorrow, but patched it carefully with some cardboard and tape to hide her wound from the outside world.

In the morning he opened the front door for business and stood behind her counter. When he phoned, the repairman said he couldn't make it in that day. At around ten o'clock a young woman with a pram paused at the door and peered in.

'Are you open?'

'Yes of course, come in.'

'Oh I just wasn't sure, because of the cardboard on the window and the lights down.' She bought the paper and a lolly for her daughter.

After she left Jimmy stared at the cardboard patch he'd stuck up so carefully the night before and wondered.

Was it really so ugly, the way they could grow old and broken together?

Acknowledgements

This story began its life as a creative writing Honours thesis, and I would like to express my thanks to my supervisor Delia Falconer for her insightful advice and ideas that contributed to this work's early development. Thank you also to Busybird for your generous help and guidance throughout this whole process. Les, your patience, thoroughness and commitment to the story has been incredible.

To the many friends, old and new, who have given me wise counsel and belly laughs, I am very thankful for your presence in my life. In particular I would like to thank Amy Tyler, Claire Dunn, Sophie Williams and Lucienne

Cassidy who helped with early drafts, and to Philippa Macaskill for her invaluable legal skills.

To my family – Mum, Dad, Claire, Chris, Leighana and AB – I am deeply grateful for your wholehearted support and encouragement of my passion for writing and creativity from my earliest moments.

Finally, thank you, Daniel. Your belief in me gave me the courage to commit to writing, your support throughout this winding process has been unwavering. You were my muse, my sounding board, and my anchor in the sea of doubt. I would not have written this book without you.

About the Author

Fascinated by humanity's deliberate blind spots, Beth Hill's passion as an anthropologist and writer is to explore and understand the places and people we leave behind in our quest for shiny new futures. From the no-man's land between the fashionable now and the romaticised past, Beth's writing is as much an exploration of our relationship to time and space as it is an archeology of intriguing character and place.

Growing up in the inner west of Sydney, a short bike ride from Parramatta Road, Beth has witnessed first-hand the mythic and mysterious places of her childhood slowly disappear. Her writing is not an act of resistance, but of remembering.

Beth studied creative writing at the University of Technology Sydney, completing her degree in Communications in 2009. Her writing has previously been published in the prestigious *UTS Writers Anthology* and the literary magazine *Seizure*. This is her first book.